I Am Thankful

By Sonali Fry

Illustrated by Alessia Girasole

A GOLDEN BOOK • NEW YORK

Text copyright © 2021 by Sonali Fry
Cover art and interior illustrations copyright © 2021 by Alessia Girasole
All rights reserved. Published in the United States by Golden Books, an imprint of
Random House Children's Books, a division of Penguin Random House LLC, 1745
Broadway, New York, NY 10019. Golden Books, A Golden Book, A Little Golden Book,
the G colophon, and the distinctive gold spine are registered trademarks of
Penguin Random House LLC.
rhcbooks.com
Educators and librarians, for a variety of teaching tools, visit us at RHTeachersLibrarians.com
Library of Congress Control Number: 2021930907
ISBN 978-0-593-42882-5 (trade) — ISBN 978-0-593-42883-2 (ebook)
Printed in the United States of America
10 9 8 7 6 5 4 3 2 1

Today we're talking about
what we're thankful for.
Are you ready? Let's begin!

I am thankful for my mama's hugs,
for crunchy leaves, and ladybugs.

I am thankful for my puppy's tricks,
my comfy slippers, and my kitty-cat's licks.

I am thankful for
my yummy lunch—
a cheese sandwich
and carrots to munch.

I am thankful for my teacher's "Hi,"
and for all her answers when I ask, "Why?"

I am thankful for the bees that buzz,
the apples we pick, and the dandelion fuzz.

I am thankful for each autumn day,
and the pumpkin patches where I play.

I am thankful for the birds that sing
as I go up, up high on my swing.

I am thankful for my grandma's pies,
her cookies, and her sweet-potato fries.

I am thankful for
my bedtime huddles,
my favorite blanket,
and Daddy's cuddles.

Now it's my turn. . . .

I am thankful for family, far and near,
and for every person I see here.

What are YOU
thankful for?